D1116225

BANANAS IN YOUR EARS

KARI YUNT

Bananas in Your Ears

Copyright © 2021 by Kari Yunt

tellwell

Tellwell Talent
www.tellwell.ca

ISBN
978-0-2288-3268-3 (Hardcover)
978-0-2288-3267-6 (Paperback)

For Mom and Uncle Will

If you were sleeping and you heard a monkey *knock knock* on the door ... would you let her in?

NO!

But why?

Because she'd put BANANAS in my EARS!

If you were sleeping and you heard a bumblebee *knock knock* on the door ... would you let him in?

NO!

But why?

Because he'd squirt HONEY on my HEAD!

If you were sleeping and you heard a pig *knock knock knock* on the door ... would you let her in?

NO!

But why?

Because she'd roll MUD all over my BED!

If you were sleeping and you heard an elephant *knock knock* on the door ... would you let him in?

NO!

But why?

Because he'd push PEANUTS up my NOSE!

If you were sleeping and you heard a mouse *knock knock* on the door ... would you let her in?

NO!

But why?

Because she'd mush CHEESE between my TOES!

If you were sleeping and you heard a gorilla *knock knock knock* on the door ... would you let him in?

NO!

But why?

Because he'd knock COCONUTS on my KNEES!

If you were sleeping and you heard
a sea lion *knock knock knock* on the
door ... would you let him in?

NO!

But why?

Because he'd slip SEAWEED
up my SLEEVES!

If you were sleeping and you heard a mommy or a daddy *knock knock knock* on the door ... would you let them in?

YES!

But why?

Because...

They'd slip the seaweed from my sleeves
And knock the coconuts off my knees.
They'd clean the cheese between my toes
And pluck the peanuts from my nose.
They'd wipe the mud off of my bed
And wash the honey from my head.

But...

They would leave the bananas there,
And in their ears they'd put a pair!

THEN WE'D ALL HAVE
BANANAS IN OUR EARS!

CPSIA information can be obtained
at www.ICGtesting.com
Printed in the USA
LVHW071235071021
699578LV00025B/279

9 780228 832683